Also by Constance W. McGeorge and Mary Whyte

SNOW RIDERS

"... a very good story ... thumbs up." —*American Bookseller,* "Pick of the Lists"

BOOMER'S BIG DAY

"Humorously sympathizing with the tribulations of moving, this endearing picture book will soothe the anxieties of children facing a move." —*Booklist*

BOOMER GOES TO SCHOOL

"The story is delightful and has a good read-aloud text.... Vivid detailed watercolors bring readers into the modern classroom." —*School Library Journal*

BOOMER'S BIG SURPRISE

"Delightful and emotionally satisfying." —*School Library Journal*

Also illustrated by Mary Whyte

I LOVE YOU THE PURPLEST by Barbara M. Joosse

"This book is a tender reminder that all children have a special place in their parents' hearts." —*Parents,* "Best Books of 1996"

For James, with love.
C. W. M.

In memory of my mother
who taught me how to waltz one night
under a full moon.
M. W.

From both of us,
thank you Jack and Pat.
C. W. M & M.W.

First paperback edition published in 2003 by Chronicle Books LLC.

Text ©1998 by Constance W. McGeorge.
Illustrations ©1998 by Mary Whyte.

Book design by Laura Jane Coats. Typeset in Goudy Oldstyle and Charlemagne.
The illustrations in this book were rendered in watercolor.
Manufactured in China.

Library of Congress Cataloging-in-Publication Data
McGeorge, Constance W.
Waltz of the scarecrows / by Constance W. McGeorge ; illustrated by Mary Whyte.
p. cm.
Summary: While staying with her grandparents on their farm,
Sarah discovers the secret behind the local tradition of dressing the
scarecrows in formal gowns and fancy coats.
ISBN 0-8118-4078-6
[1. Scarecrows—Fiction.] I. Whyte, Mary, ill. II. Title.
PZ7.M478467Wa1 1997 [E]—dc21 97-1347 CIP AC

Distributed in Canada by Raincoast Books
9050 Shaughnessy Street, Vancouver, British Columbia V6P 6E5

10 9 8 7 6 5 4 3 2 1

Chronicle Books LLC
85 Second Street, San Francisco, California 94105

www.chroniclekids.com

WALTZ
OF THE
SCARECROWS

by Constance W. McGeorge ❧ illustrated by Mary Whyte

chronicle books · san francisco

S arah awoke with a start. A loud noise shook the ceiling above her head. She threw back the quilt, jumped into her overalls, and was heading for the attic when she heard Grandma calling her downstairs for breakfast.

The scent of pancakes and maple syrup filled the kitchen.

"What's that noise in the attic?" Sarah asked her grandmother.

"Oh, that's just Grandpa," Grandma began to explain. But before she could say more, Grandpa appeared. He was carrying a large bundle of clothes.

"Good morning, Sarah," he said. Then, he marched straight through the kitchen and out the back door. "I'll be in the barn," he called out as the screen door closed behind him.

"What's Grandpa doing?" asked Sarah.

"You'll see," Grandma answered with a smile. "But first, let's eat our pancakes."

Sarah hurried through breakfast then found Grandpa in the barn. He was sorting through the bundle of clothes from the attic.

Sarah watched him carefully unfold a man's evening coat with tails. Shaking out the wrinkles, he laid the coat down gently. Then, he straightened the brim of a shiny top hat. Next, he unwrapped a blue satin gown.

The sleeves of the coat were patched, and the gown had faded from a dark indigo to a sun-bleached blue. But still, they were the most beautiful clothes Sarah had ever seen.

"Sarah, my dear," Grandpa announced, "the crops are full and harvest is near—it's time to make scarecrows!"

"But I thought scarecrows only wore raggedy old clothes," said Sarah.

"Not *our* scarecrows!" answered Grandma. With her sewing basket in hand, Grandma sat down on a milking stool and set to work mending a tear in the faded blue gown.

Grandpa untied a bale of straw and began stuffing the old clothes. Sarah helped, buttoning buttons and filling sleeves and gloves with straw. Then, she and Grandma braided yarn for hair and sewed it around faces made of old pillow cases.

Finally, Grandma placed the top hat on the head of one scarecrow, and Sarah placed a hat with silk flowers on the head of the other.

As Sarah helped Grandma and Grandpa carry the scarecrows into the cornfield, she noticed a pair of scarecrows in the field across the road. One was wearing a black topcoat and the other a bright red ball gown. In the neighbor's garden, she saw another pair of scarecrows dressed in fancy clothes, too.

"Grandpa," Sarah cried, "all the scarecrows are dressed up!"

Grandpa sat down on an old tree stump and motioned to Sarah to sit beside him. "Why, it's a tradition here," he said. "It all started one summer long ago."

"That year, we had the best crops we'd ever seen. The corn grew a foot taller than usual, and there were more pumpkins on the vines than we could count. Even the sunflowers were brighter that year than anyone could remember.

"To celebrate our bounty, a harvest ball was planned. Folks sent away to the city for fancy clothes—evening coats and top hats, ball gowns and high-heeled shoes. The town was decorated with garlands and lanterns, and an orchestra came all the way from Riverton to play.

"At dusk, on the night of the ball, we dressed up in our fine new clothes and strutted into town. We were so excited, we didn't even notice the dark cloud approaching from the west. As the orchestra began to play and we started to dance, the cloud came closer and closer.

"As it turned out, it wasn't a dark cloud
at all. It was a swarm of hungry birds, and they
were after our crops!

"Screeching and cawing, the birds picked
at the corn, pulled at the beans, and poked at the
pumpkins. The orchestra stopped playing, and we
ran into the fields, shouting and shaking our fists.

"Well, those birds took one look at our black coats flapping and our colorful dresses billowing, and they took flight back into the evening sky!

"We must have been a sight, running through the fields, our fancy clothes flashing in the twilight. Luckily, our food for the coming year was saved. But worry was on everyone's mind. What would we do if the birds returned?

"Without a word, we knew what
we had to do. We hurried home and
changed into work shirts and overalls.
We cleaned our coats and mended our
gowns, and then we stuffed them all with straw.

"One by one, under the rising moon, the fanciest
scarecrows anyone had ever seen began to appear in
the fields. And, do you know what? The birds stayed
away. And they have stayed away every year since,"
Grandpa concluded.

"But there's more to the story," said Grandma,
her voice nearly a whisper. Sarah moved closer to hear
every word.

"Some folks say that when the crops are full and the harvest moon rises in the sky, a wind blows in from the south. The cornstalks sway, and the faint sound of music drifts through the fields.

"Others say they've heard the sounds of rustling satin, coattails flapping, and a shuffling that lasts long into the night."

"There are even a few," Grandpa added, "who claim they've *seen* the scarecrows waltzing."

Then, Grandpa and Grandma took
Sarah by the hand, and together they
twirled around and around.

One night, after Sarah had returned home from her summer visit to Grandpa and Grandma's farm, she sat at her bedroom window. Outside leaves rustled on the trees, and the full moon hung low in the sky. Sarah had an idea.

She opened the closet and took out her old velvet party dress. Just then, a soft knock sounded at her bedroom door. Her mother peeked in.

"This dress is too small for me," said Sarah. "I'm going to send it to Grandma and Grandpa."

"What are your grandparents going to do with an old party dress?" asked her mother.

Sarah smiled. She knew Grandma and Grandpa would know just what to do.

A NOTE FROM THE AUTHOR

When I visit schools, students ask how I think of story ideas. I often start with something I love—and I love fall! It's my favorite time of year. The leaves on the trees turn beautiful, brilliant colors, and the cooler weather is a nice change after a long, hot summer. Fall is also the time of year that we see the scarecrows. These wonderful straw folk pop up everywhere to protect field crops and vegetable gardens—but sometimes they're put up just for fun. So you can see that when I set out to write *Waltz of the Scarecrows* I was able to combine many things that I love in just one story.

I've had a wonderful time reading this story to school children, and I've been amazed at how generously teachers and students have been willing to share ideas and projects that have come from exploring this book. With their help, I've gathered together many ways that you can enjoy *Waltz of the Scarecrows* to the fullest.

Connie McGeorge

A NOTE FROM THE ILLUSTRATOR

Connie and I had already created several picture books together when she shared this story with me. I felt a special connection with it right from the start. You see, I also love scarecrows, and when I was young my mother, a ballet dancer, taught me how to waltz one night under the moonlight!

When I began the illustrations for the story, I decided to hide a scarecrow in the background on each page of the story. For instance, if you look at the very last illustration you'll see a cat sitting on a fence. But look a little closer. Can you see the silhouette of a scarecrow on the cat's back? Have fun finding the others!

Mary Whyte

A GUIDE TO USING THIS BOOK

As you read this book aloud, allow time for everyone to look closely at the illustrations. Children will enjoy pointing out the elegantly dressed scarecrows, and of course, the hidden scarecrows cleverly concealed in each illustration. *Waltz of the Scarecrows* can then be used to initiate discussion on a variety of issues, including seasons, traditions, legends, and imagination, as well as special relationships like the one Sarah and her grandparents share.

WRITING EXERCISES

- Fall is the author's favorite time of year. What is your favorite time of year? Why do you like that season best? What are some of the fun things you like to do during that season?

- In this story, the farmers wore fancy clothes to the Harvest Ball. When have you worn fancy clothes?

- The scarecrows in this story, according to the legend told by Grandma and Grandpa, like to waltz in the field under the harvest moon. Finish the following sentence with a story:
If I were a scarecrow, I would …

- Pretend there is a dance or special occasion coming up. Make an invitation to send to all the guests. Be sure to include such information as the day, the time, the place, and what to wear.

INTERDISCIPLINARY PROJECTS FOR TEACHERS AND PARENTS

Oral Language or Discussion Topics

- The main character, Sarah, learns about the scarecrows on a summer visit to her grandparents' farm. Ask students to discuss their memories of a trip or family visit.

- The last page of the book does not have any words on it. Explain in your own words what happened after Sarah sent her old party dress to Grandma and Grandpa.

Music

- Ask children to listen to a waltz, then ask them to name other types of music. Discuss which characteristics distinguish a waltz from other music.

Dance

- Show children the dance steps used in a waltz, then ask them to name other kinds of dances. Discuss which characteristics distinguish a waltz from other dances.

Art

- Did your readers find all the hidden scarecrows in the story illustrations? Discuss the different ways Mary Whyte hid the scarecrows and have children create "hidden scarecrows" in their own drawings.

- Mary Whyte used watercolor paints to create the illustrations in this book. What other materials could be used to create a picture of a scarecrow?

Community Service

- The author once visited a school while the staff and students were conducting a food drive. They collected food under a large poster of a scarecrow and the message below read "Scare off hunger." Ask children to think of different ways in which to help their community that tie into the story.

While visiting her grandparents' farm one summer, Sarah helps her grandma and grandpa make scarecrows. Together they stuff old clothes with straw and sew button eyes onto pillow faces. But these are no ordinary scarecrows. Dressed in top hats and tails, ball gowns and gloves, these scarecrows look as if they are ready for a night on the town. And, indeed, they are!

Coupled with sweeping watercolor illustrations that almost glow with moonlight, this magical tale will set readers' imaginations dancing.

"From the endpaper of golden straw to the final spread, the text and illustrations are sure to win the hearts of children." —*School Library Journal*

Smithsonian Magazine 1998 Notable Books for Children

Selected as "Outstanding" in *Reviews from Parent Council, 1999*

Constance W. McGeorge was born and raised in Ohio and lives there today with her husband, Jim, and their two dogs. She was inspired to write *Waltz of the Scarecrows* by her love of scarecrows and autumn, dancing and dressing up.

Mary Whyte is an accomplished artist best known for her watercolor paintings. She grew up in Ohio, where every autumn she made scarecrows. She now lives in South Carolina with her husband, Smith Coleman.